OLD HAT

NEW HAT

OLD HAT NEW HAT

by Stan
and Jan
Berenstain

COLLINS

1234   K L

Old hat.

Old hat.

New hat.

New hat

New hat

New hat

New hat

Too big.

Too small.

Too flat.

Too tall.

Too loose.

Too tight.

Too heavy.

Too light.

Too red. Too dotty.

Too blue. Too spotty.

Too fancy.

Too frilly.

Too shiny.

Too silly.

Too
beady.

Too
bumpy.

Too
leafy.

Too
lumpy.

Too
holey.

Too
patchy.

Too
feathery.

Too
scratchy.

Too
crooked.

Too
straight.

Too
pointed . . .

WAIT!

Just right!

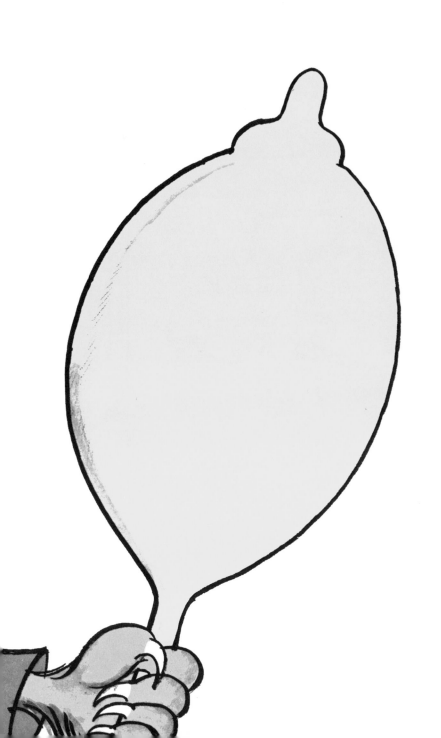

New hat.

Old hat.